Dear Parent:
Your child's love of r

Every child learns to read in a different way and at his or her own speed. Some go back and forth between reading levels and read favorite books again and again. Others read through each level in order. You can help your young reader improve and become more confident by encouraging his or her own interests and abilities. From books your child reads with you to the first books he or she reads alone, there are I Can Read Books for every stage of reading:

SHARED READING
Basic language, word repetition, and whimsical illustrations, ideal for sharing with your emergent reader

BEGINNING READING
Short sentences, familiar words, and simple concepts for children eager to read on their own

READING WITH HELP
Engaging stories, longer sentences, and language play for developing readers

READING ALONE
Complex plots, challenging vocabulary, and high-interest topics for the independent reader

ADVANCED READING
Short paragraphs, chapters, and exciting themes for the perfect bridge to chapter books

I Can Read Books have introduced children to the joy of reading since 1957. Featuring award-winning authors and illustrators and a fabulous cast of beloved characters, I Can Read Books set the standard for beginning readers.

A lifetime of discovery begins with the magical words **"I Can Read!"**

Visit www.icanread.com for information
on enriching your child's reading experience.

I Can Read Book® is a trademark of HarperCollins Publishers.

Marmaduke: Meet Marmaduke

Library of Congress catalog card number: 2009943954
ISBN 978-0-06-199505-7

Typography by Rick Farley

10 11 12 13 14   LP/WOR   10 9 8 7 6 5 4 3 2 1   ❖   First Edition

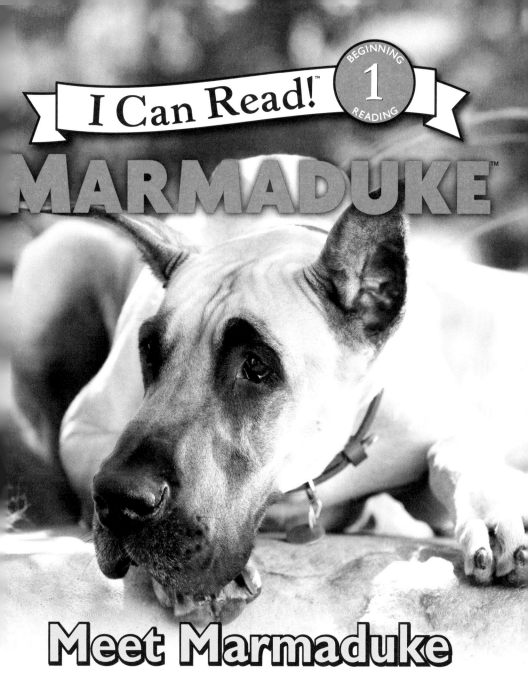

I Can Read!

BEGINNING 1 READING

MARMADUKE

Meet Marmaduke

Adapted by Kirsten Mayer

Based on the comic created by
BRAD ANDERSON and PHIL LEEMING

Written by
TIM RASMUSSEN & VINCE DI MEGLIO

HARPER

An Imprint of HarperCollinsPublishers

Meet Marmaduke.
He is a very big dog.

Marmaduke is so big
that when he rides in a car,
his head sticks out
from the roof!

When Marmaduke takes a bath,

he only fits in a human bathtub.

He is so tall that he can grab
a snack off the counter.

When he wants a drink,

Marmaduke slurps water from the toilet.

He just moved to California.

Marmaduke likes his new house.

It is bigger than his old home.

A big dog needs a lot of space.

Marmaduke wants to play.

He digs a hole in the yard,

but he gets bored quickly.

His only friend is Carlos the cat.

But it's hard for a big dog

to play with a small cat.

Marmaduke needs more friends.

He goes to the dog park

to meet all the dogs in town.

Will he find a new friend?

Marmaduke sees many little dogs.

They whisper when he walks by.

"Wow, he's huge!"

"I've never seen a dog that big!"

Marmaduke feels sad.

Is he too big

for anyone to like him?

Just then a large black dog

walks up to Marmaduke

along with two smaller dogs.

"I'm Bosco," says the black dog.

"My name is Marmaduke.
You can call me Duke,"
says Marmaduke.
Maybe Bosco will be his friend!

"Let me tell you how it is,"
says Bosco.
"If you cross into our turf,
you will be sorry."

"Yeah, steer clear, horsey!"

shouts one of the smaller dogs.

They are not friends,

they are bullies!

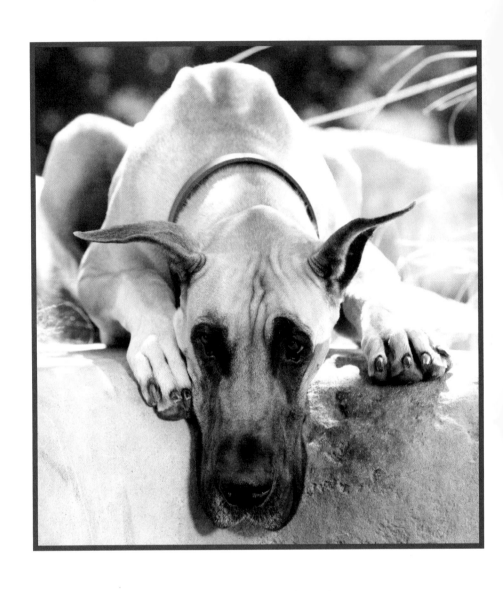

Marmaduke is crushed.

He will never find a new friend!

He sits on a rock all alone.

Three smaller dogs appear
and sniff the air around him.
The one wearing a bandana says,
"What's your name, newbie?"

"I'm Mazie," the dog continues.

"This is Raisin and Giuseppe."

Raisin wears a bow tie.

Giuseppe has funny hair.

"I am Marmaduke," he answers.

"Good to meet you.

Do you come here a lot?"

He tries to be nice.

"We are here all the time,"

says Mazie.

"But so is Bosco."

"Forget Bosco," says Raisin.

"Ignore him," adds Giuseppe.

"You can hang with us,"
says Mazie.
"We are having a party tonight.
You should come."

Marmaduke's ears perk up.

"Really? That sounds cool."

"See you tonight!" says Mazie.

Marmaduke is excited.
He might have found
some new friends!

That night, he sneaks out
and goes to Mazie's house.
Marmaduke is a little nervous.
"Is this the party?" he asks.

"Marmaduke is here!"
shouts Raisin.

"Welcome!" says Mazie.

"Come on in."

Giuseppe plays a dancing game.

"I just beat my own record!

Who wants to play next?"

Marmaduke laughs.

"I'll sit this one out."

Mazie brings out a toy cow.

"This is for you," she says.

"It is my favorite toy to chew."

Marmaduke looks at Mazie
and says, "I think it's cool.
Thank you."
Mazie smiles.

Mazie, Raisin, and Giuseppe meet

Marmaduke at the dog park

the next day and every day after.

Marmaduke is happy.

These dogs are his best friends.